DATE DUE

JY 12			
AG 27			
			PRINTED IN U.S.A.

The Storm

Akiko Miyakoshi

Kids Can Press

It's Friday.
My parents promised to take me to the beach tomorrow.

But earlier, our teacher told us,
"Be sure to go straight home after
class. There's a bad storm coming."

I've been looking forward to our trip to the beach all week!
   But every time I look at the sky, it gets darker and darker ...

My parents prepare for the storm, closing the shutters tight and bringing the flowerpots inside.

I just mope.

"If we can't go tomorrow, we'll go next week," my mother says.

I don't want to go next week. I want to go tomorrow.

I hear rain pattering on
the roof and peek outside.
The storm!

All through dinner, the rain
beats hard against the shutters.
The wind howls and blows.
I try not to be scared.

What was that noise?!
I jump into bed.

When I pull the blankets over my head,
the rain gets quiet.

I wonder how fast the wind blows.
I wish I had a ship with big propellers
that would spin stronger winds to drive
the storm away.

The ship sails into the black clouds.
I keep watch.

I climb up to the crow's nest,
just before the ship is swallowed
by the darkness.

I can't see a thing.
The propellers keep turning.

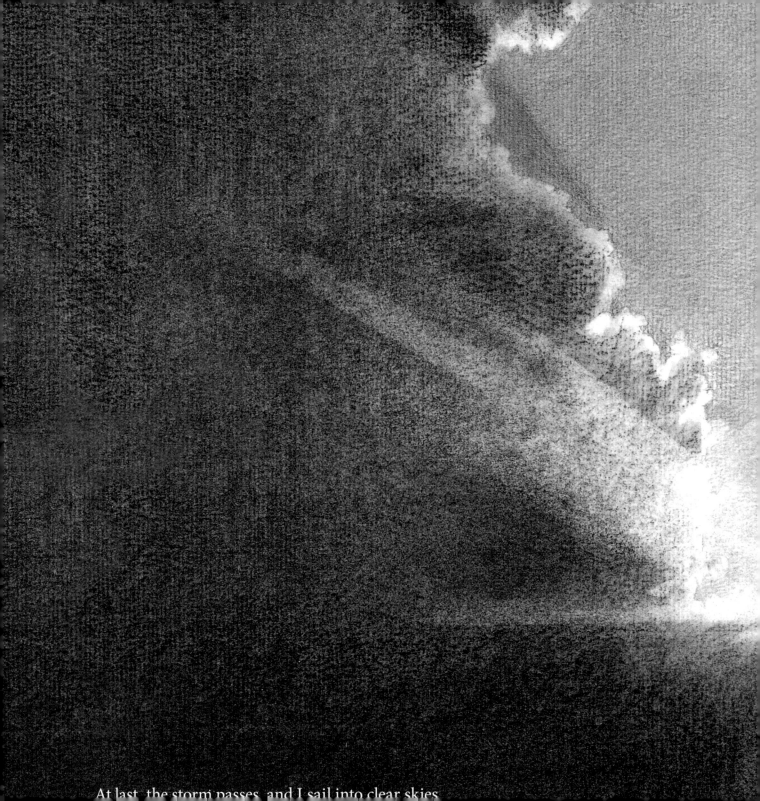

At last, the storm passes, and I sail into clear skies.

In the morning, sunshine
streams through my window.

Perfect for a day at the beach!

First published by Kids Can Press in 2016

Taifû ga Kuru
Copyright © 2009 Akiko Miyakoshi
First published in Japan in 2009 by BL Publishing Co. Ltd., Kobe

English translation rights arranged with BL Publishing Co. Ltd.
through Japan Foreign-Rights Centre
English translation © 2016 Kids Can Press

Kids Can Press acknowledges the financial support of the
Government of Ontario, through the Ontario Media Development
Corporation's Ontario Book Initiative.

Published in Canada by   Published in the U.S. by
Kids Can Press Ltd.   Kids Can Press Ltd.
25 Dockside Drive   2250 Military Road
Toronto, ON M5A 0B5   Tonawanda, NY 14150

www.kidscanpress.com

English edition edited by Yvette Ghione and Katie Scott.

This book is smyth sewn casebound.
Manufactured in Shenzhen, China, in 10/2015 by C & C Offset.

CM 16 0 9 8 7 6 5 4 3 2 1

Library and Archives Canada Cataloguing in Publication

Miyakoshi, Akiko, 1982–
    [Taifû ga kuru. English]
    The Storm / Akiko Miyakoshi.

Translation of: Taifû ga kuru.
ISBN 978-1-77138-559-6 (bound)

    I. Title. II. Title: Taifû ga kuru. English.

PZ7.M682St 2016   j895.6'36   C2015-903363-2

Kids Can Press is a *Corus* Entertainment company